To my delightful daughter, Sonia,
and the squash she loved—P.Z.M.

For Ariane Goetz—A.W.

Visit us on the Web! randomhouse.com/kids

Educators and librarians, for a variety of teaching tools, visit us at RHTeachersLibrarians.com

*Library of Congress Cataloging-in-Publication Data*
Miller, Pat Zietlow.
Sophie's squash / Pat Zietlow Miller ; [illustrations by] Anne Wilsdorf. — 1st ed.
p. cm.
Summary: A young girl befriends a squash.
ISBN 978-0-307-97896-7 (hc) — ISBN 978-0-307-97897-4 (glb)
[1. Squashes—Fiction. 2. Friendship—Fiction.]  I. Wilsdorf, Anne, ill. II. Title.
PZ7.M63224 So 2013
[E]—dc23
2012006438

The text of this book is set in Hoefler.
The illustrations were rendered in watercolor, ink, and China ink.
Book design by Rachael Cole

MANUFACTURED IN CHINA
10 9 8 7 6 5 4 3 2 1

First Edition

# SOPHIE'S SQUASH

WRITTEN BY **Pat Zietlow Miller**

ILLUSTRATED BY **Anne Wilsdorf**

schwartz **&** wade books · new york

**O**ne bright fall day, Sophie chose a squash at the farmers' market.

Her parents planned to serve it for supper, but Sophie had other ideas.

It was just the right size to hold in her arms.

Just the right size to bounce on her knee.

Just the right size to love.

"I'm glad we met," Sophie whispered.

"Good friends are hard to find."

At home, Sophie used markers to give her squash a face.
Then she wrapped it in a blanket and rocked it to sleep.

When it was time to make supper, Sophie's mother looked at the squash.
She looked at Sophie.

"I call her Bernice," Sophie said.

"I'll call for a pizza," said her mother.

After that, Bernice went
everywhere with Sophie.
To story time at the library.

To visit other squash at
the farmers' market.

To practice somersaults by the garden.

Every night, Sophie gave Bernice a bottle, a hug, and a kiss.

"Well, we did hope she'd love vegetables," Sophie's mother told her father.

"Shhhhhh," Sophie said. "Bernice is sleeping."

"Sweet pea," Sophie's mother said one morning as they made blueberry waffles, "Bernice is a squash, not a friend. If we don't eat her soon, she'll get mushy and gross. Let's bake her with marshmallows. Won't that taste yummy?"

"Don't listen, Bernice!" Sophie cried.

That afternoon, Sophie's father took her shopping.

"Sugar beet," he said, "Bernice is a squash. Why
don't you pick a nice toy to play with instead?"

But the trucks were too hard,

and the dolls were too soft.

Sophie clutched Bernice tightly.
"No thanks," she said. "I have
everything I need."

After supper, Sophie's parents called a Family Meeting. Bernice napped in Sophie's lap.

"Why don't we donate Bernice to the food pantry before she rots?" her father suggested.

Sophie shook her head. "Bernice will last forever."

"Bernice seems a little blotchy," said Sophie's dad on the

way to the library one day.

"She looks perfect to me," Sophie replied.

At story time, some kids pointed and stared.

"What's that spotty thing?" a boy asked.

"Her name is Bernice, and she's a SQUASH," Sophie said. "With FRECKLES."

"Maybe Bernice should stay home next time," Sophie's mom suggested.

"Why?" Sophie asked. "She wasn't the one being rude."

Still, as winter neared, Sophie noticed changes.
Bernice seemed softer, and her somersaults lacked
their usual style.

"Visiting friends will cheer you up," Sophie said.

At the farmers' market, squash were everywhere.

Firm, shiny squash.

"What keeps a squash healthy?" Sophie asked a farmer.

"It's simple, really," he said. "Fresh air. Good, clean dirt.
A little love."

*Well*, Sophie thought. *I have all that.*

At home, Sophie cleared leaves from Bernice's favorite spot. She made a bed of soft soil, tucked Bernice in, and kissed her good night.

"Get better soon," she whispered.

That night, while Sophie slept, the wind whistled
and tiny snowflakes fell.

When she awoke, the world was covered in white.

"Do you think Bernice is cold out there?" Sophie asked her mother.

"I'm sure she's warm and cozy under her snow blanket," her mother replied.

Sophie gazed out the window all morning.

She was still there in the afternoon when
her father came home with a surprise.
"You need a new friend," he said.

"Meet Ace!"

Ace was nice, but boring.
He just swam around and
around in his bowl.

But during the long winter, Sophie discovered that Ace was a superb silent reader who did fabulous flip turns. And he always listened politely when she talked about Bernice.

When the snow finally melted, Sophie rushed to the garden.

The only thing there was a small green sprout.

It looked strangely familiar.

"Bernice!" Sophie said. "How was your winter?"

After that, Sophie, Ace, and Bernice ate lunch
together every day.

One bright summer morning,
Sophie somersaulted across her yard,

landed by the garden,
and stared in disbelief.

Bernice had grown two tiny squash.

"Wow!" Sophie told them. "You look just like your mom!"

Soon, Bonnie and Baxter were just the right size for
Sophie to hold in her arms and bounce on her knee.

Just the right size to love.